The Lion's Paw

By Jane Werner Watson
Illustrated by
Gustaf Tenggren

A Golden Book • Nev

ISBN: 0-307-96008-0
www.goldenbooks.com
PRINTED IN CHINA   First Random House Edition 2002

Ow! roared the lion. "There is a thorn in my paw. Who will take it out?"

"Not I," said the solid rhinoceros.
"I am sharpening my pointed horn."

"Not I," said the startled kudu.
"I am racing away from here!"

"Not I," whispered the tall giraffe among the tip-top leaves.

"Not I," said the bouncing baboon.
"I am having too much fun."

"Who will take the thorn out?"
asked the crowned crane.

"Not I," said the hippopotamus.
"I am cooling off in the mud."

"Not I," said the striped zebra.
"I am kicking up my heels."

"Not I," said the bright-eyed monkey.
"I am swinging by my tail."

"Not I," said the big gorilla.
"I am scratching away my fleas."

"Not I," said the elegant gazelle.
"I am leaping across the veld."

"Will no one remove the thorn?"
called the ibis by the purple pool.

"Not I," said the slippery crocodile,
smiling a hungry smile.

"Not I," said the trumpeting elephant.
"I am taking a shower."

"Not I," said the spotted leopard.
"I am slinking through the shade."

"Not I," said the solemn buffalo.
"I have too much work to do."

"Who will help the lion?" cried the ostrich running over the desert sands.

"Not I," said the swooping vulture.
"I'm busy hunting a meal."

"Not I," said the fast cheetah.
"I'm busy hunting, too."

"I will," said the little mouse.
And she did!